WELCOME TO

RAVENS PASS

CHEATERS

by Steve Brezenoff
illustrated by Amerigo Pinelli

Ravens Pass is published by Stone Arch Books
a Capstone imprint
1710 Roe Crest Drive
North Mankato, Minnesota 56003
www.capstonepub.com

Cataloging-in-Publication Data is available at the Library of Congress website.
ISBN: 978-1-4342-4616-5 (library binding)
ISBN: 978-1-4342-6216-5 (paperback)

Summary: Three friends cheat on a math test and get away with it — until a strange substitute teacher starts asking questions.

Graphic Designer: Hilary Wacholz
Art Director: Kay Fraser

Photo credits:
iStockphoto: chromatika (sign, back cover); spxChrome (torn paper, pp. 7, 13, 21, 37, 33, 41, 49, 55, 63, 69, 75, 81) Shutterstock: Milos Luzanin (newspaper, pp. 92, 93, 94, 95, 96); Robyn Mackenzie (torn ad, pp. 1, 2, 96); Tischenko Irina (sign, pp. 1, 2).

Printed in China by Nordica
1114/CA21401814
112014   008621R

Between where you live and where you've been, there is a town. It lies along the highway, and off the beaten path. It's in the middle of a forest, and in the middle of a desert. It's on the shore of a lake, and along a raging river. It's surrounded by mountains, and on the edge of a deadly cliff. If you're looking for it, you'll never find it, but if you're lost, it'll appear on your path.

The town is **RAVENS PASS,** and you might never leave.

TABLE OF CONTENTS

Chapter 1

ONE LITTLE TEST

"It'll be fine, Andrew," said Jimmy.

Jimmy, Andrew, and Mia leaned on the lockers across from room 212 of Ravens Pass Middle School. It was Wednesday morning, and seventh-grade math class was about to start.

Mia sighed. "Seriously, Andrew," she said. "We're talking about one test. One little, tiny test."

"That's easy for you to say," Andrew replied. "You two are probably failing math, anyway."

"Hey!" said Jimmy. "I have a solid C-minus."

Andrew ignored him. "But I'm running a perfect A," he said. "If we get caught, I'll probably end up with an F."

"Or get kicked out of school," Mia said.

Andrew's eyes went wide. "Kicked out?" he said in a whisper.

"Stop it, Mia," said Jimmy, pulling Andrew aside. "She's just kidding. Besides, we're talking about Mrs. Huckle here. She won't catch us."

Andrew sighed. "Are you sure?" he asked.

Jimmy put up his right hand. "I promise," he said.

"Okay," Andrew said. "Then let's do it."

They took their regular seats in the back of the classroom.

Mrs. Huckle distributed the exam papers. She stood at the front of the room, pushed her glasses up her beak-like nose, and tightened her cardigan.

"Is everyone ready?" she asked in her high-pitched voice. Then she checked the skinny watch on her freckled wrist. "You have exactly forty minutes to finish this exam." She smiled over the sea of young faces.

Mia glanced at Jimmy. Jimmy glanced at Andrew. Andrew glanced at Mia. He nodded.

"Begin," Mrs. Huckle said. All twenty-five students began the exam.

* * *

Forty-five minutes later, the three back-row kids left room 212. "That went perfectly," said Mia. "You were great, Andrew."

Andrew shrugged. "It was a tough exam," he said. "I think I did well."

Jimmy put one arm around Andrew's shoulders. "Of course you did," Jimmy said. "You're a genius at math. Everyone knows it."

"And now Jimmy and I are geniuses too," Mia said with a giggle.

Andrew glared at her. "We just better not get caught," he said.

Mia waved him off. "Mrs. Huckle didn't have a clue," she said. "She was too busy reading that romance novel."

"I hope you're right," said Andrew.

"She is, she is," said Jimmy. He guided Andrew down the hall. "Now come on. I'll buy you lunch."

Chapter 2

A-PLUS

The next morning, Mia, Jimmy, and Andrew filed into room 212.

Mrs. Huckle was widely known as the quickest grader at Ravens Pass Middle School. She always got tests and quizzes back the next day. There was just one problem: that day, she wasn't at school.

The substitute teacher stood at the front of the room. He was the oddest sub any of the kids had ever seen. His hair was the color of very dry grass right before winter, and it was far too long.

The sub's hair looked like it hadn't been brushed in days. His big mustache was also raggedy. His shirt was bright yellow, and his jacket was green and red plaid. His short, wide tie was black with green polka dots.

Jimmy leaned over close to Mia and Andrew. "Who is this guy?" he whispered. "I thought I knew every sub this school ever hired."

Mia shrugged. But Andrew smiled — if Mrs. Huckle was absent, she couldn't accuse them of cheating. Maybe he didn't have anything to worry about after all.

"Boy and girls, ladies and gentlemen," said the substitute. "And anyone else here today."

A few students chuckled.

"I am Sir Godfrey Kong Windham McCaw," the sub said in a very serious and important voice.

Then the sub bowed. His tie flopped up and hit him in the face, but he didn't seem to care. It was a very deep bow. When he stood upright again, he added, "You may call me Mr. Smith."

"That didn't make any sense," whispered Jimmy.

Mia just shook her head.

Mr. Smith held up his bag. "I have your exams here," he said. "Mrs. Huckle was kind enough to grade them all last night, despite being sick. I picked them up from her house this morning."

The new teacher turned his bag upside down over the desk at the front of the classroom. Exam booklets fell out like an avalanche, covering the desk in a mess of blue and white paper.

"There we are," said Mr. Smith. "Now, please come and collect your graded exams." He stepped to the side. None of the students moved.

Mr. Smith clapped twice, loudly. "Don't dawdle," he said. "Come up and take your exams."

Jimmy glanced at Andrew and Mia. He shrugged, then pushed his chair back. It squeaked loudly. He walked toward the front of the room.

"Ah!" said Mr. Smith. "I was hoping you might be brave enough to go first, Mr. Duncan."

Jimmy stopped halfway up the middle aisle. "How did you know who I was?" he asked.

Mr. Smith grinned. His big mustache bent into a hairy half moon. "How could I not?" he said. Without looking, he reached into the pile of exams and pulled one out. Then he held it up. "Jimmy Duncan, you earned an A-plus."

Jimmy's eyes went wide and he grabbed the exam. "Wow," he said.

"Yes," said Mr. Smith. "Now, who's next?"

Jimmy walked back to his desk. Mia leapt up from her seat. "I'm next," she shouted, hurrying to the front.

"I knew it!" said Mr. Smith. He pulled out another test, again without even looking. "Mia Plank: A-plus!"

Mia pumped her fist. "Yes!" she said, grabbing the exam. "Thanks, Mr. Smith."

The substitute teacher howled with laughter. "You're quite welcome!" he said. "And speaking of 'thanks,' why don't you come get your paper, Mr. Floyd."

He whipped a booklet out from behind his back and held it up. "Come now, no surprises here," he said. "An A-plus for Andrew Floyd."

Deftly, Mr. Smith folded the booklet into a crude paper plane. Then he sent it soaring to the back of the room. It landed squarely on Andrew's desk. There it was, in red ink: $A+$.

"As for the rest of you," Mr. Smith said, his smile gone now, "Mrs. Huckle was disappointed."

The whole class turned to face Andrew, Jimmy, and Mia.

"In fact," Mr. Smith added, "no one else got better than a C."

Everyone glared at the three in the back row. Andrew slid down in his chair. He wished he could just disappear.

Jimmy leaned over. "Stop acting so weird," he whispered. "It worked. We all aced the exam."

Behind Andrew's back, Mia and Jimmy high-fived and smiled.

Chapter 3

A STRANGE VISITOR

After supper that night, Mia sat and watched TV with her parents. Her father, full of fried chicken, dozed in the big easy chair. Mia's mother knitted. Mia stretched out on the rest of the couch with the remote in her hand.

She flicked through the channels quickly. "There's nothing worth watching," she said.

"How can you can tell?" her mom asked without looking up from her knitting. "You never stop long enough on any channel to see what anything is."

The doorbell rang. Mia's father snored. Her mother's needles clicked and clacked.

Mia sighed. "Fine," she said. "I'll get it."

She got up from the couch and headed toward the front door. The doorbell rang again.

"I'm coming, I'm coming," Mia said. "Sheesh."

Mia pulled open the door. "What do —" she started to say. Then she froze. It was Mr. Smith.

"Good evening, Ms. Plank," he said. "I hope I haven't come at a bad time."

"N-no," Mia said. "Um, is something wrong?"

Mr. Smith put one hand on his chest. "Wrong?" he said. "Why, what in heaven's name could be wrong?"

"I don't know," said Mia. "It's just that a substitute teacher hasn't come to my house before."

"Well, you need not worry, my dear," Mr. Smith said. He reached into the inside pocket of his jacket. He pulled out a gold ribbon and held it out to her. "A special award!" he said.

It occurred to Mia that Mr. Smith always seemed to be making a speech. He never just said anything. He only announced and pronounced things, almost like he was performing for everyone.

Still, she reached out and gingerly took the ribbon. It had a big smiling face on it, along with the words, "Most Improved."

Mr. Smith placed one hand on his heart. "As recognition of your place as the most improved student in Mrs. Huckle's math class," he said, "I present you with this award." He smiled at her.

"Um, thanks," Mia said.

From behind her came the sudden sound of clapping. Her parents were right behind her.

"We're so proud, Mia," her mother said.

"I didn't even know you had an exam," said her father.

Mia did her best to smile, but it came out crooked.

"Is something wrong, Mia?" said Mr. Smith, leaning closer to her. "You seem nervous."

Her parents leaned in close too.

"No, everything's fine," Mia said. "I mean, everything's great." She held up her ribbon and forced a big smile. "I'm just excited, is all."

Mr. Smith left, and her parents went back to the living room to watch TV. Mia went to her bedroom and locked the door.

She made a quick phone call to Andrew. He hadn't gotten a visit from Mr. Smith. Then she called Jimmy and asked him.

"No," Jimmy said. "Just a normal night around here. No weird subs showing up at our doorstep."

"Weird," said Mia. "Your grade in math has improved as much as mine has, right?"

"Probably," said Jimmy. "So what?"

Mia took a deep breath. "I don't know," she said. "Something about this sub just isn't quite right."

"He's just a weird guy," Jimmy said. "Don't let it get to you."

"Okay," said Mia. "See you tomorrow."

She clicked off her phone and lay back on her bed. But she couldn't get the image of Mr. Smith's grinning face out of her mind.

Chapter 4

BAD DREAMS

Jimmy put down his phone. Mia and Andrew were getting too nervous. They'd each called him that night, worried that Mr. Smith knew they'd cheated. But that was ridiculous. The sub hadn't even been in the room when they took the test.

Jimmy shrugged it off and began to get ready for bed. Tomorrow morning, they'd be back in class, and Mr. Smith would probably be gone.

* * *

Jimmy woke up to total darkness. He turned his head and looked at the clock. It read 3:30 a.m.

Jimmy's throat was dry. It was like a desert had moved into his mouth. He threw back the blanket and stood up. "Water," he said to the darkness. He groped through the darkness toward the kitchen.

He didn't get far. In the hallway outside his room, Jimmy stopped. Something had moved downstairs. He went to the top of the steps as quietly as he could. He got down on all fours to try to see the floor below. A light flickered in the kitchen. Someone had just opened the fridge.

Probably just Dad, Jimmy thought. *Sneaking another piece of that cake Mom made on Sunday.*

Jimmy went back to his bedroom. When he got there, the desk lamp was on. Sitting at the desk, holding a glass of ice water, was Mr. Smith.

"Good evening, Jimmy," the sub said. "Thirsty?"

Jimmy screamed.

Mr. Smith laughed. His mouth grew impossibly huge as he cackled and tossed his crazy hair.

Jimmy ran for his parents' room. A lamp clicked on as he opened the door. Mom and Dad were sitting up in bed, reaching for their glasses.

"What's going on?" Dad said. "Are you okay?"

"Someone's in my room," Jimmy said, running to his father. He grabbed his father by the hand.

Dad's face grew worried. He put on his glasses and hurried down the hall.

Jimmy and his mom waited. A minute passed. Then Dad called out, "Come on in here," he said.

Mom and Jimmy went down the hall to Jimmy's room. Dad was sitting on the edge of Jimmy's bed, holding the flashlight.

"No one's here," Dad said.

"What?" Jimmy said. He moved slowly into the room. He pulled open the closet door. Just clothes. He got down on his knees to check under the bed. Just dust — and a lone sock.

"He was here," Jimmy said.

"Who was?" asked Mom.

"Mr. Smith," said Jimmy. "The math sub."

Dad chuckled. "You just had a bad dream," he said. He stood up and put a hand on Jimmy's shoulder. "Go back to sleep."

Jimmy leaned against his bed as his parents left his room. The glass of ice water was gone. *Then it was just a dream,* he thought.

But then he saw something. In the middle of the desk was a shiny circle. He ran his finger through it. His finger came back wet.

Chapter 5

CREEP

"I'm telling you," said Jimmy quietly. "It really happened."

Jimmy, Andrew, and Mia were huddled together in the back of room 212. There were still a few minutes until class would start.

Mia shook her head slowly. "Sure sounds like a bad dream to me," she said. "Not that I blame you. That Mr. Smith is creepy with a capital C."

Andrew nodded excitedly. "I had a nightmare about him too," he said.

"This was no nightmare," said Jimmy.

"Come on," said Andrew. "You really think our substitute math teacher broke into your house in the middle of the night?"

"It's possible," said Jimmy.

Mr. Smith stepped up behind them. "Good morning, A-plus students," he said. He put a firm hand on Andrew's shoulder. "What are we discussing this fine Friday morning?"

"Nothing, Mr. Smith," Mia said quickly.

"Nothing?" Mr. Smith said, grinning. "Three great minds like you? Nonsense. You're probably talking about some mathematical theorem! Share it with me, won't you?"

Jimmy forced a laugh. "No, really," he said. "We weren't talking about anything interesting."

"Be modest if you like," said Mr. Smith. He pulled up a nearby chair and joined their huddle. "But I'll get the truth out of you yet."

The three friends exchanged a glance. Mr. Smith smiled at them, one by one. His lips curved up his cheeks. His teeth were broad and yellow. His eyebrows angled sharply. His eyes squinted as his smile grew larger. Soon, it was impossibly big.

The room around the three friends began to grow dark. All they could see was Mr. Smith's face. His grin, growing larger and larger. His teeth, becoming bigger and yellower and sharper. His eyes, glowing red in the dark classroom.

The giant grin opened wider and wider. Mr. Smith began to laugh. It was a thin, horrible laugh. It wormed into Andrew's ears. It wiggled down Jimmy's spine. It crawled through Mia's hair.

The laughter grew louder and louder. Andrew couldn't take it anymore. He clapped his hands over his ears. "Stop it," he cried. "Stop it!"

And then it was over. The room was bright again. The laughter stopped. Mr. Smith's grin had vanished. In fact, now Mr. Smith was at the front of the room. Several math problems were written on the whiteboard.

"Stop what, Mr. Floyd?" Mr. Smith asked. "Has one of my prized students found an error with my calculations?" His lips formed the slightest smile.

Andrew blinked hard. "No, sir," he said.

"Then I'll continue the lesson," said Mr. Smith.

* * *

A few minutes later, the bell rang. Mia, Andrew, and Jimmy hurried out of the classroom.

They walked fast down the hall toward the cafeteria. Their faces were pale with fear.

"What just happened in there?!" Mia asked.

"He's not normal," said Andrew.

Jimmy shook his head. "He can't be human," he said.

"He's a monster," said Andrew. "A demon."

"Calm down," said Mia. She hopped in front of the two boys to be first in line for food. "He's not a demon. We're all just a little freaked out."

"Freaked out?" said Jimmy. "Did you see what I saw back there?"

"Seriously," said Andrew, nodding. "He's nuts."

Mia glanced at the food behind the glass. It was lasagna day. "He's just a substitute teacher," she said, then added, "Okay, and he's a little weird."

"That's the understatement of the decade," muttered Andrew.

"And today is Friday," added Mia. "So he can't bug us over the weekend. And Mrs. Huckle will probably be back on Monday too. The end."

"How do you know he won't bug us?" said Andrew. He added a cup of pudding to his tray. "He went to your house last night, didn't he?"

Mia shrugged. "If he shows up again, I won't invite him in," she said, taking a plate of lasagna.

"What about what happened to me?" said Jimmy. "You don't think I invited him in at three in the morning, do you?"

Mia rolled her eyes. "That was obviously a dream, Jimbo," she said.

Jimmy grunted, but he didn't argue. His friends thought he was crazy enough already.

Chapter 6

ANDREW'S SATURDAY NIGHT

Saturday night arrived quickly. By the time Andrew got to his room after supper and started his homework, he'd mostly forgotten about Mr. Smith and the math exam.

Then he pulled out his math book. He didn't have any homework — subs almost never assigned homework — but he wanted to look over the material. Andrew was the top math student in his grade, and he wanted to keep it that way.

Andrew opened his math workbook and grabbed his pencil. Just as he started to work, the desk lamp flickered.

"Piece of junk," Andrew muttered. He tapped the bulb with his finger and it flickered again. Then it flashed brightly and went dark.

"Great," he said. He got up from his desk and walked to the door. "Mom," he called out. "I need a new bulb for my desk lamp."

No one answered. "Mom!" he shouted.

Still, no one answered. He went back into his room and moved his books to the bed. He switched on the bedside lamp. Then he grabbed his pencil, lay down, and started to work.

He was halfway through the first problem when the light next to him flickered again. It flashed brightly, and then went dark.

"Are you kidding me?" he said to no one in particular. He fiddled with the lamp's switch. The bulb lit up, brighter and brighter, until he had to shade his eyes. Luckily his hand was in front of his face, because an instant later, the bulb exploded.

Tiny shards of glass flew in every direction. The lamp smoldered. A small flame now flickered where the bulb had been.

Andrew screamed. He blew on the lamp, trying to put out the fire. Then he jumped up and pulled the lamp's power cord from the wall. The lamp smoked and fell over, smashing against the hardwood floor.

"That was nuts," Andrew said quietly. Then he yelled, "Dad, the lamp broke!"

Andrew grabbed his math books and headed to the kitchen to work under the bright ceiling fixture.

As Andrew started down the steps, he called out again, "Dad? Did you hear me?"

No one answered. "Where is everyone?" Andrew said. He went into the kitchen. The light over the table worked, and the row of three small lights over the counter worked too. He opened the fridge to get a juice box, and even the light in there worked.

Andrew sat at the kitchen table and opened his math workbook. When he picked up his pencil, the pages of the book began to flip, slowly at first, and then quickly — too quickly to even stop them. It was like a fan was blowing the pages along. But there was no breeze in the room.

He slapped his hands onto the book to stop the pages. The book fluttered under his hands, like a wild animal trying to break free of his grasp.

"Help!" Andrew shouted. "Mom! Dad!"

He jumped up from his chair and the book took off like a bat, flapping its pages, zipping back and forth. Andrew huddled into the corner and covered his head with his arms.

Finally the book dove at him. It slammed into his body, and then fell to the floor.

Andrew didn't move. He waited, eyeing the book carefully, making sure it wouldn't attack again. It seemed like he was huddled there forever, holding his breath, watching the book.

After a few minutes, the book still hadn't moved. Slowly, Andrew reached for it. He flinched as the corner of the cover fluttered slightly. Then he grabbed it in both hands.

The moment he did, it burst into flames.

Chapter 7

MIA'S SATURDAY NIGHT

Mia was sitting on the couch, watching TV in her living room. Her parents were out. It was one of their "date nights." Mia and her older brother were home alone. Mia's brother, Jonah, was a great babysitter. He just went to his room, closed the door, and played video games. That meant Mia had a solid five straight hours in front of the TV with full control over the remote.

Mia flipped quickly through the channels while she sipped her can of soda.

Mia heard a light switch in the next room, and figured it was her brother. Then the light flicked off in the TV room. "Jonah, is that you?" she asked without looking up.

No one answered, but a great horror movie was starting on a movie channel. Mia soon forgot all about the light flicking off.

* * *

Halfway through the horror movie, the TV screen went black.

"Um," Mia said, "what happened?" She mashed the power button on the remote, but the TV wouldn't switch on. The room was dark.

"Jonah!" Mia called. She grunted as she walked to the TV to try hitting the main power button. But just before her fingertip touched the power button, the TV flashed back on.

The show on TV was not the horror movie she had been watching. This one was in black and white, and it looked like an old sitcom.

There was a man in an old-fashioned living room, muttering to himself. He was wearing an apron over his nice pants and shirt and tie, and seemed to be getting ready for a dinner party.

"Oh my, oh my," the man said nervously. "So much to do!"

The audience laughed and laughed, but Mia stared at the TV in horror. A chill ran down her spine. The man in the show wasn't just some old actor from the 1950s. It was Mr. Smith, the math sub.

"Let's see," he said, tapping his chin. "I've set the table, made the soup, sent the invitations . . ."

His jaw dropped.

"Did I send the invitations?" he said in a quiet, deep voice. The audience laughed hysterically. He began to sniff the air. "What is that strange smell?"

The audience giggled. They knew what was coming. "The roast is burning!" Mr. Smith shouted, running for the kitchen.

The kitchen was filled with smoke. Mr. Smith quickly pulled on his mitt and yanked open the oven. Thick, black smoke poured out. Mr. Smith coughed, and the audience laughed.

"Oh, no!" he said. "It's ruined."

The camera zoomed in on the oven once the smoke had cleared. The audience gasped.

In the center of the oven, sitting in a roasting pan, was Mia's head.

Mia screamed.

Chapter 8

JIMMY'S SATURDAY NIGHT

Jimmy Duncan was in his basement, practicing his electric guitar. He wasn't very good yet. As he strummed, every chord sounded flat or sharp. Nothing sounded right.

But he wanted to be great someday, so he kept practicing. He strummed until his fingers hurt.

His mother didn't approve. "If you practiced math like you practiced guitar," she reminded him constantly, "then you wouldn't be doing so poorly in school."

"I'll show her," Jimmy muttered to himself. "I'll get so good at the guitar, I won't need math. I'll become a rock star and make millions."

He was practicing the chords for one of his favorite songs when the amp began to crackle. He strummed a little harder. It crackled even louder.

"Must be a loose wire," he said. He knocked the side of the amp with his hand. It echoed and boomed, then went silent.

Jimmy strummed his guitar, harder and harder, and the amp crackled and echoed.

"It actually sounds kind of cool," he said. He strummed even harder, and then flinched.

"Ow," he said, dropping his pick. The strings had cut his fingers. With his left hand, he pressed on the guitar strings to silence them, and he flinched again as a jolt of electricity hit him.

"What's with this thing?" he shouted, tossing the guitar to the floor. It landed with a thump, and the amp echoed and crackled. Harsh feedback filled the basement. It grew louder and louder.

Jimmy flicked the power switch to shut it off, but nothing happened. The echo grew louder still. He pulled the plug from the wall, but it had no effect. The feedback swelled and whirled around him. He ran for the door. It was locked.

"What?!" he cried, but he couldn't even hear his own voice over the feedback from the amp. "This door doesn't even have a lock on it!"

He ran back to the amp and kicked it with all his might. But it didn't work. With each kick, the amp seemed to find a new pitch for its feedback. Soon the noise was so loud that Jimmy thought that his ears might bleed. That he might go deaf.

But deep in the awful sound, he heard something familiar. A man's voice. He strained to listen, to make out the words: the voice was reading a math problem. "That's Mr. Smith's voice," Jimmy said.

A pounding came from the basement door. *It's Mr. Smith!* Jimmy thought. *He's trying to get in.*

Jimmy ran to the door and pushed against it. "Go away!" he shouted. "Leave me alone!"

But a voice called back. He could barely hear it over the deafening feedback and math formulas coming from the amp. It wasn't Mr. Smith out there. It was a girl's voice.

Jimmy pulled and tugged at the door. It wouldn't budge. He looked around in a panic and grabbed his guitar. Then, holding it like a hammer, he let out a great battle cry.

Then Jimmy brought the guitar down on the front of the amp as hard as he could. The boom was even louder than the feedback.

Then there was silence.

The basement door flung open. Mia ran in. "Jimmy!" she said. She looked like she'd been crying. "What's going on?"

He just shook his head and opened his mouth, but he couldn't think of a single way to explain.

"We have to call Andrew," Mia said. She tossed him her cell phone.

Jimmy nodded, dialing Andrew's number. Andrew was breathless. "Hello?" Andrew said. "Hello?"

"Andrew," said Mia. "It's me. I'm at Jimmy's. Something very weird is going on."

"It's not weird," said Andrew. "Mr. Smith is a demon. He's going to kill us."

Mia took a deep breath. "I don't know if he's a demon," she said. "But obviously he's creepy, and he knows we cheated."

"So what do we do?" Andrew said. "Run away?"

Jimmy took the phone from Mia. "We should go talk to Mrs. Huckle," he said. "We should confess that we cheated on her test."

Chapter 9

CONFESS

Andrew left his house immediately. It was late, but they had to confess right away to Mrs. Huckle in person. It didn't seem like the kind of thing you could do over the phone.

When Andrew knocked on Mrs. Huckle's door, it opened. There was Mrs. Huckle. She wore a heavy bathrobe and carried a box of tissues. Her nose was red.

"Andrew," she said, her voice nasal. "What are you doing here?"

Andrew didn't speak right away. He was a little surprised that Mrs. Huckle had answered the door. He'd half expected Mr. Smith to answer it.

"Please come in," Mrs. Huckle said, stepping aside. Andrew walked in. He sat on the little couch in the front room.

"Would you like some tea?" Mrs. Huckle asked, standing in the doorway. "I've just made a pot."

"No, thank you," said Andrew, wringing his hands. "Um, Mia and Jimmy are on their way over."

"Mia and Jimmy?" she said. "What is this about?"

Andrew glanced at the big clock hanging over the window. What was taking them so long?

His hands were sweating. "I should really wait for them," he said.

Mrs. Huckle sat down next to him.

She patted his shoulder. "Andrew, tell me what's wrong," she said. "I'm certain I can help."

"We cheated!" Andrew blurted out. He jumped up from the couch. "I let Mia and Jimmy see all my answers to the big exam last week and they copied them all and that's why we got A-plusses!"

Mrs. Huckle was about to interrupt, but Andrew kept rambling. "That's why they got A-plusses, I mean," he added. "I studied hard, so I didn't cheat, except that I helped them cheat —"

"Andrew!" said Mrs. Huckle, putting up her hands to quiet him. "I'm surprised you're involved with something like this."

He looked at the floor. "I know," he said quietly.

"But wait," Mrs. Huckle said. "Where are Mia and Jimmy? You said they were on their way here."

Andrew nodded. "We thought if we told you everything, then Mr. Smith would leave us alone."

"Who is Mr. Smith?" Mrs. Huckle asked, arching her eyebrows.

Andrew was confused. "The sub," he said. "For your math class. You don't know about him?"

Mrs. Huckle shook her head.

"We thought you sent him after us," Andrew said. "You know, like you knew we cheated, and he was going to get revenge for you."

Mrs. Huckle squinted. Then her face went pale. "Mia and Jimmy are on their way here?" she asked in a frightened voice.

"Yes," Andrew said.

"Come with me," Mrs. Huckle said, pulling him toward the steps. "Your friends are in terrible, terrible danger."

Chapter 10

THE ATTIC

Mrs. Huckle dashed up the attic steps. The whole way, she never let go of Andrew's wrist. He half ran, and was half dragged upstairs. When they reached a musty attic, she finally let go of him to turn on a lamp.

Andrew gasped. "What is this place?" he asked.

The attic was mostly empty, but in the center was a large, round table. Candles of all different sizes covered the table. Some were half burned down. Others looked new. In the middle was a big, leather-bound book.

She hurried to the book and flipped through the pages. "Here it is," Mrs. Huckle said. "'Protection from cheaters.'"

"You did this?" Andrew asked quietly. He backed up slowly, planning to take off down the steps. "Then we were right. Mr. Smith is a demon, and you summoned him to get your revenge on us!"

"Not at all," Mrs. Huckle said in her most pitiful voice. "I never meant for this to happen."

"Then what did you intend?" Andrew said.

"My car broke down," she said. "The mechanic charged me so much money to fix it that I wanted to make sure he wasn't cheating me. I didn't think the spell would apply to my students too."

Andrew crossed his arms. "Well, it did," he said.

Mrs. Huckle nodded. "Then we have to break the spell," she said.

"How?" said Andrew. His voice was angry.

"I'm trying to find it," said Mrs. Huckle. "This isn't easy, you know. It's not written in English."

Andrew sighed and went to the little window. He looked out over the moonlit streets of Ravens Pass and hoped his friends were almost there.

Chapter 11

THE SPELL

"Can't you walk any faster?" Mia said. She jogged ahead of Jimmy, pulling him along.

"I'm tired," he said. "It's late. I shouldn't even be out right now. My folks are going to kill me."

"A demon wants to torture and kill us," Mia said, "and you're worried about getting in trouble?"

Jimmy shrugged.

"Just hurry," Mia said, jogging faster.

Suddenly, Mr. Smith was standing in front of them. He had appeared, it seemed, out of thin air.

"Where are you two going at this late hour?" Mr. Smith said. He was wearing his most ridiculous outfit yet, and was smiling his big, evil smile.

They stopped and stared.

"Let us by," said Mia, mustering all the bravery she could. "We're going to talk to Mrs. Huckle."

Mr. Smith clucked his tongue. "At this hour of the night, you two are going to bother a poor, sick, old woman?" he said. "That sounds about right, for a couple of dirty cheaters like you two."

"We're going to confess," said Jimmy. "We're going to tell her we cheated on the math exam, so she can forgive us. Then you can go back to whatever evil dimension you came from."

Mr. Smith clapped. "Bravo," he said. "How very honest of you. But it's too late, I'm afraid. I have been summoned to do a task, and I will fulfill the contract."

From behind his back, he produced a small black book. In gold lettering, the words on the front read, "THE RULES."

"Now let's see," Mr. Smith said. "What is the appropriate punishment for cheating on math tests?"

He flipped through the pages, sometimes stopping to lick his fingertip.

"We're not waiting around to find out," Mia whispered to Jimmy. "Let's get out of here while he's distracted."

They turned to run.

Without looking up, Mr. Smith called out through his big smile. "Not so fast, you two."

He snapped his fingers. Mia and Jimmy instantly found themselves wrapped in iron chains and hanging from a lamppost.

"Now I've lost my page," Mr. Smith muttered. He started again at the front.

Chapter 12

THE END

Andrew was growing impatient. Mrs. Huckle had been paging through the book for several minutes now, looking for a way to break the spell.

"Please hurry up," he pleaded.

"Ah!" said Mrs. Huckle. "I think I've finally found it. It says, 'To break the spell, the cheater must confess.'"

"I have confessed!" said Andrew. "So why isn't the spell broken?!"

"I don't know," said Mrs. Huckle, tapping her chin. "Maybe Mia and Jimmy have to confess too."

"They're on their way here now," Andrew said excitedly. He headed for the steps. "Come on, they'll probably be here any minute."

"I don't know," Mrs. Huckle said. "It says here that the demon won't give up easily."

"What do you mean?" Andrew said.

"Mr. Smith doesn't want to go back to his dimension," said Mrs. Huckle. "He wants to stay here, so he can continue to punish cheaters."

"Then he won't want them to confess," said Andrew. "He'll try to stop them."

Mrs. Huckle nodded gravely.

Andrew darted down the steps. "Hurry up!" he called behind him. "You'll have to drive."

"I can't!" Mrs. Huckle said, following him downstairs. "Remember? My car isn't running!"

Andrew and Mrs. Huckle ran along Main Street for several minutes. "There they are!" Andrew called.

Mia and Jimmy were hanging from a lamppost, wrapped in thick, iron chains. Below them was a huge bubbling cauldron. Next to the cauldron, Mr. Smith slowly paced back and forth. He was still grinning, and still flipping through the rule book. He read all the various punishments out loud in his booming voice.

"Eaten by alligators," he said. "Drowned in hot lava. Buried alive in flesh-eating worms . . . this is a very tough choice, indeed!"

"Help us!" Mia called out.

"Please get us out of here!" Jimmy screamed.

Andrew put his hands to his mouth like a megaphone. "We can't help you," he cried. "To free yourself, you must —"

"I don't think so," Mr. Smith interrupted. Andrew hadn't even realized he knew they were there. "You are the third cheater. You must be punished as well."

Andrew's eyes went wide. Next thing he knew, he was in chains too, hanging right next to his friends. A steel muzzle covered his mouth.

Mrs. Huckle stomped toward the demonic substitute teacher. "Set them free!" she demanded. "I summoned you, and I can banish you too!"

Mr. Smith laughed, and then continued reading aloud. "Dropped from the highest mountain in the world into a lake of acid? No, something else," he said with glee. "Maybe eaten alive by piranhas?"

Mrs. Huckle stepped past the demon and right up to the base of the lamppost. She shouted up Mia and Jimmy. "You must confess!" she said.

"But you already know!" Mia cried out.

Mrs. Huckle screamed. "Confess — now!"

Jimmy didn't wait. "We cheated!" he said. "We're sorry! We really are!"

Mia nodded. "We're so sorry," she said. "We cheated and we're really sorry!"

Mr. Smith stopped reading. "No fun," he said. The book slapped shut by itself and then he slipped it into his back pocket. He snapped his fingers and the cauldron vanished, along with the chains. All three children fell to the sidewalk.

"Ow," said Mia. She stood up, rubbing her shoulder where it had hit the ground.

"Maybe next time," Mr. Smith said. "I have a feeling these three aren't done cheating just yet."

He snapped his fingers again. A black portal opened up behind him. Without turning around, he stepped through it. The last part of him that vanished was his sinister grin. Then the portal blinked out of existence.

Mrs. Huckle took all three of her students in her arms. "There now," she said.

"We're sorry, Mrs. Huckle," said Andrew. "We'll all take the test again."

"Yes, you will," she said. A smile crawled across her face that none of the three friends noticed.

ABOUT THE AUTHOR

STEVE BREZENOFF lives in Minneapolis, Minnesota, with his wife, Beth, and their son, Sam. Besides writing books, he enjoys playing video games, riding his bicycle, and helping middle-school students to improve their writing skills. Steve's ideas almost always come to him in his dreams, so he does his best writing in his pajamas.

ABOUT THE ILLUSTRATOR

A long time ago, when AMERIGO PINELLI was very small, his mother gave him a pencil. From that moment on, drawing became his world. Nowadays, Amerigo works as an illustrator above the narrow streets and churches of Naples, Italy. He loves his job because it feels more like play than work. And each morning, as the sun rises over Mount Vesuvius, Amerigo gets to chase pigeons along the rooftops. Just ask his lovely wife, Giulia, if you don't believe him.

GLOSSARY

AMP (AMP)—an amplifier, or a device used to make the sound coming from a guitar louder

CARDIGAN (KAR-duh-gun)—a knitted sweater or jacket that fastens down the front

CAULDRON (KAWL-druhn)—a large, rounded cooking pot

CHORD (KORD)—a combination of musical notes

MODEST (MOD-ist)—not boastful or proud

MUSTY (MUHSS-tee)—if something or someplace is musty, it smells of damnpness, decay, or mold

THEOREM (THEER-uhm)—a statement, especially in mathematics, that can be proved to be true

VANISHED (VAN-ishd)—disappeared without a trace

DISCUSSION QUESTIONS

1. Re-read the last page of the story in this book. Do you think Mrs. Huckle knows more than she claims? Why or why not?

2. In this series, Ravens Pass is a town where crazy things happen. Has anything spooky or creepy ever happened in your town? Talk about stories you know.

3. Who is more to blame for summoning the evil substitute teacher — Mrs. Huckle, or the three friends? Explain your answer.

WRITING PROMPTS

1. What happens next? Write a short story that extends this book.

2. Have you ever cheated at something? Write about a time when you cheated, or bent the rules.

3. Write a newspaper article describing the events in this book. What do the three friends have to say about the recent events?

THE CROW'S

SPELL-ING ERROR?

Today I bring you an interesting story straight from the mouths of three Ravens Pass teens. They claim that Mrs. Huckle, their math teacher, cast an evil spell that summoned a demon to Ravens Pass in a misguided attempt to punish a cheating car mechanic. But instead of getting a refund, Mrs. Huckle got more than she bargained for.

Instead of solving Mrs. Huckle's car-related woes, the demon attempted to punish these three students for cheating on one of Mrs. Huckle's math tests. The kids claim they narrowly escaped from the demon by confessing their crimes, but can't produce any solid evidence of what happened. Strangely, Mrs. Huckle has been completely silent about the odd events. It seems suspicious to me that she wouldn't deny the claims

EYE

outright — that is, if there wasn't any truth to the kids' claims.

So, readers, what do you think? I know I've made up my mind: this teacher's hiding something, that much is obvious.

So I turn to you, my clever readers. What do you think really happened? Was there a demon running amok in Ravens Pass, or did three cheating students just add lying to their crimes? Email me.

Did this teacher summon a demon to our demension?

MORE DARK TALES